green kids club ™

In the
Andes
Mountains
of Chile

chilean mines

Written by Saige J. Ballock-Dixon and Sylvia M.
Illustrations by Joy Eagle

Special thanks to Jim Sanderson

Green Kids Club Adventures
(Also available in Junior-First Reader Editions)
The Green Spring (First Story)
Ice Jams
Coral Reef
Jade Elephant
Gorilla's Roar
Desert Mirage
Chilean Mines
Wolf Howls
The Elephant and the King

Aventuras del Club de Niños Verde
El Manantial Verde (Primera Historia)
Barreras de Hielo
Arrecifes de Coral
El Elefante de Jade
El Rugido del Gorila
El Espejismo del Desierto
Las Minas Chilenas
El Aullido del Lobo
El Elefante y el Rey

Medina, Sylvia M. / Ballock-Dixon, Saige J.
chilean mines / by Sylvia M. Medina & Saige J. Ballock-Dixon; Illustrated by Joy Eagle. -2nd ed.
ISBN: 978-1-939871-34-3
Audience: Ages 5-9
Summary: The Green Kids travel to Chile, South America to visit their friend Natalia. The kids are feeling lucky as they go to see the local mines, but an earthquake and endangered Andean Cat make it more of an adventure.
1. Endangered Species. 2. Wildlife Rescue.
3. Wildlife Reintroduction. 4.Nature Conservation.
591.68 - Rare & Endangered Species   2014936911

green kids club

Published by Green Kids Club, Inc., P.O. Box 50030, Idaho Falls,ID 83405

For the little animals.
Each animal, big or small,
has an important role in the world.

Victor and Maya are known as the Green Kids because they help the environment. They have traveled to Chile to visit their pen pal, Natalia. They wanted to go hike and explore the mountains of Chile. Natalia had told them all about the wonders of her country - the beautiful forests and jungles, mighty rivers and amazing animals.

Natalia greeted Victor and Maya with a big hug. She had spent the entire day planning their hiking trip in the mountains and was eager to take the Green Kids exploring.

After they finished unpacking they headed into the mountains. As the kids started hiking they noticed that some of the rocks sparkled in the sunlight. Victor and Maya asked Natalia, "What are all those beautiful sparkles in the rocks?"

Natalia replied, "My country is beautiful inside and out! Inside the beautiful rocks are gold, copper, and jewels. This is what makes our mountains shine!" As Natalia said this, she reached up and touched a special pair of gold earrings her grandmother had given her.

7

As they hiked along Natalia told them that they would not only be seeing an old Chilean mine, but they may also be able to see the elusive Andean Cat.

Maya said, "Tell us more about this cat."

"Well Maya," said Natalia, "there are very few of these cats left in this country. They are endangered and have a hard time finding each other in the wild. There is a legend about one of these cats living in this part of the jungle, and she is supposed to be BIG. We call her "Gato de la Suerte"- lucky cat. There are very few Andean Cats left and she is the biggest cat in our mountains. Legend says that just seeing her will give you fortune and good luck."

The Green Kids hiked deeper into the mountains and came to a clearing that had mines in the mountain side.

Maya peered into the mine shaft, "Where does this lead to?"

Natalia said, "That mine goes into the center of the mountain where we can search for copper, gold, and jewels."

Victor asked, "Why are there so many mines? Can we go into one?"

Natalia answered, "There are many mines because everyone wants the beautiful minerals found in them. My Mom and Dad do not want me to go into the mines, because they say they are dangerous. But I guess we could, just this once."

12

The kids grabbed the head lamps that were sitting at the entrance of the tunnel and started into the mine shaft. The kids were happy to have lights on their hats because the mine was very scary and dark! But, they were all determined to find some treasure in the mine.

As they crawled through the narrowing shaft they heard a rustle out in front of them. They looked towards the noise and caught a glimpse of two eyes peering at them. Could it be Gato de la Suerte?

As they started to climb over the rocks towards the eyes, they felt the earth begin to shake. It felt like an earthquake. "Run!" shouted Natalia.

The kids started running towards the entrance of the cave when suddenly, Natalia fell through a crack in the floor board and into a pool of water below.

Maya and Victor peered down through the boards and saw Natalia sitting in the middle of a beautiful blue green spring. She was wet from head to toe and had accidently swallowed a mouth full of water when she fell in. Maya and Victor realized that this was the same spring that gave children the power to talk with animals!

"Please help me," cried a little voice. Natalia turned to see who was talking. It was an Andean Cat, and he was stuck under some old boards.

Natalia could understand the cat. She looked up at Victor and Maya in amazement. "Wow, that is the Andean Cat that I was telling you about. I just heard the cat talking, did you hear him?"

"You have gained the power of the Green Kids," Maya said to Natalia.

Natalia looked toward the cat, "Are you Gato de la Suerte?"

The cat replied, "People call me that, but my name is Camilo. I have been looking for other cats like me. All of a sudden, Camilo started crying, "I am so lonely!" He yowled. "I can't find anyone else like me anywhere. I am starting to think there are no more of my kind left."

Maya reached over and softly touched him. Camilo looked up, his eyes brimming with tears. He said, "I thought I saw a girl cat come into this shaft so I tried to follow her in here, but my paw got caught and I have been stuck in here for days. Can you help me?"

The Green Kids began clearing the boards away from Camilo. They freed his paw and then they began heading towards the entrance of the shaft.

19

All of a sudden the earth started shaking again. The kids realized that they were in an earth-quake and started running out. Rocks started falling from above.

Victor and Natalia made it out of the mine shaft just in the nick of time. They turned to look for their friends, but they could not see them. Maya and Camilo had been trapped inside.

Victor heard shouting from inside the cave, "Camilo and I are okay, but you must find help, or we may never get out of here," yelled Maya.

Victor said, "We will go get help. Hang on!" Victor and Natalia started running up the trail as fast as they could.

Suddenly an Andean Cat jumped down from the rocks in front of them.

"Camilo?" Victor questioned.

The cat replied, "No, my name is Sofia, I thought I saw another Andean Cat in this area and I have been searching for him."

Natalia gasped, "We know where he is, but he is trapped with our friend. We are going to find help."

"I can help!" shouted Sofia as she ran back to the blocked mine shaft with Victor and Natalia following behind.

As they reached the blocked mine shaft, Sofia called out, "Stand back," and she pushed the rocks with all her might. Magically, the rocks began to move. Victor and Natalia joined in to help too. They pushed together until a small opening cleared that Maya and Camilo could fit through.

Maya crawled through the opening with Camilo behind. They were covered in dust.
    Camilo looked up and saw Sofia. He couldn't believe his luck - another Andean Cat and she was so beautiful, he couldn't help staring at her. He had been searching for so long.

Natalia was in shock at the sight of the two Andean Cats, "I can't believe my eyes, two Lucky Cats!"

"We are very lucky. Thank you, Sofia. Without your help, Camilo and I would be trapped in that mine shaft," said Maya.

Habitat - the area in which an animal or plant normally lives or grows.

"What can we do to repay you?" Natalia asked.

"Teach others about Andean Cats and not to continue taking us, otherwise there will not be any of us left in this world. Also, help to protect our land, we need healthy mountain habitat so we can survive," answered Camilo.

28

"Of course," replied Natalia, "we will teach others around the world about protecting our lands and maybe one day Andean Cats will no longer be endangered."

The Green Kids turned to head back to Natalia's home while the Andean Cats bounded away into the mountains of Chile.

Maya, Victor, and Natalia knew the legend of Gato de la Suerte was true,
he had brought the children good luck.

A New Family!

andean cat facts

The Andean Mountain Cat is about the size of a housecat, but looks bigger due to its thick fur and fuzzy tail.

They live in the high Andean mountains of South America in four countries - Bolivia, Argentina, Peru and Chile.

© Jim Sanderson

© Jim Sanderson

Very little is known about the Andean Cat - it is thought to be one of the rarest of felines.

Many people who live around the Andean Cat think the cat has special powers and brings good luck. Local people have been known to catch them and use their coats to bless their crops and livestock.

There are less than 2000 cats in the wild. The main issues that the Andean Cat faces are thought to be habitat disturbance, hunting, reduction of prey, and small population size.

The Andean Cat is protected in all four countries that it inhabits.

Vicuña is a relative of the Llama and Alpaca. They live in the Andes Mountains at very high altitudes. It has extremely fine wool.
Vicuña are protected by law, but were once endangered.

Guanaco is also a relative of the Llama and Alpaca. They are an Andes Mountains native and are wild. The Guanaco uses it's excellent running ability to avoid pumas. Guanaco are protected by law.

Viscacha live in rocky regions. Viscacha eat Yareta and other lichens. They are hunted for both meat and fur.
The Viscacha population is declining.

science section

The best methods for protecting the Andean Cat are to learn more about the cat and teach local communities about the it. Protecting vital habitat and food sources will also help the Andean Cat.

Extinction - a species no longer exists.

Andean Cat

Guanaco

Vicuña

Yareta

Viscacha

The Andean Cat is nearing extinction.
Once an animal becomes extinct it is gone forever.

Each animal plays an important role in its ecosystem.
An ecosystem is the living and non-living things that work together to make a balanced unit.
The extinction of an animal greatly impacts the balance of life. For example:

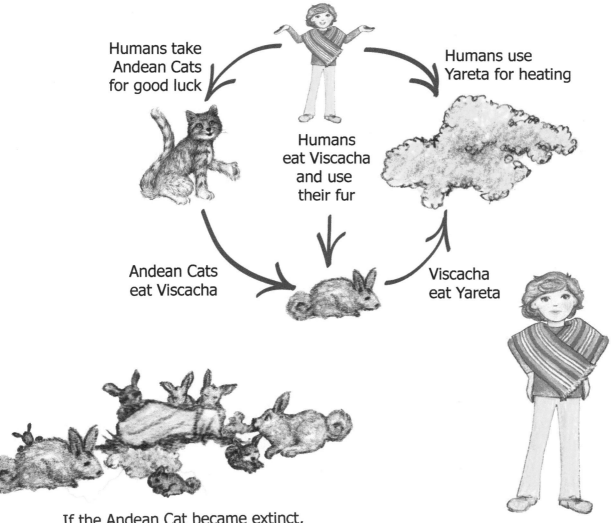

Humans take
Andean Cats
for good luck

Humans use
Yareta for heating

Humans
eat Viscacha
and use
their fur

Andean Cats
eat Viscacha

Viscacha
eat Yareta

If the Andean Cat became extinct,
for a while there would be lots of Viscacha.
But then the Yareta would be eaten all up
and the Viscacha would not have enough food.

And then the humans would not have
Yareta to keep them warm and
Viscacha to eat.

Removing animals in the ecosystem can make the entire ecosystem off balance.

9 781939 871343